Unicorn Academy™

SOPHIA'S INVITATION

nosy crow

First published in the UK in 2023 by Nosy Crow Ltd
Wheat Wharf, 27a Shad Thames,
London, SE1 2XZ

Nosy Crow Eirann Ltd
44 Orchard Grove, Kenmare,
Co Kerry, V93 FY22, Ireland

Nosy Crow and associated logos are trademarks
and/or registered trademarks of Nosy Crow Ltd

ISBN 978 1 80513 100 7

ENTERTAINMENT

A CIP catalogue record for this book is available from the British Library.

Printed and bound in Great Britain by Clays Ltd, Elcograf S.p.A.
Typeset by Tiger Media

Papers used by Nosy Crow are made from wood grown in sustainable forests.

13 5 7 9 10 8 6 4 2

www.nosycrow.com

PROLOGUE
A JOURNEY BEGINS...

In the furthest corner of the bluest ocean, through secret shoals and hidden behind an enchanted mist, lies the most amazing place on Earth. Every part of it tingles with magic – from the sparkly, snow-capped mountain peaks to the flower-strewn forests. This is Unicorn Island.

One day, a twinkling dot of magenta light appeared in the island shadows. Quick as a hummingbird, the light darted out into the sunshine, flitting left and right. It shimmered and circled above the island's waterfalls and meadows, before gliding up towards a green hilltop. An opal-white unicorn with a spiralled horn was standing there, gazing out across the sea.

The unicorn watched, her rainbow mane billowing in the breeze, as the dot danced closer and closer. She was not startled – it was a light she had seen many times before. The dot swirled around the body of the majestic creature, along her horn and up into the air. It was a Fate Fairy, a tiny magical being with fluttery pink wings and bright eyes. The unicorn silently bowed her head in greeting. The Fate Fairy hovered beside the unicorn for the shortest of moments then flew off once again, spiralling up, up into the sky ... where it joined a cloud of other Fate Fairies glowing in gem-like colours, their wings buzzing with excitement.

SOPHIA'S INVITATION

The unicorn looked up to see the Fate Fairies gather and then soar higher still. Just before they disappeared out of sight, the cloud suddenly separated, the dots whooshing off in different directions. All that was left behind was the beautiful unicorn and a fading glow of shimmering, pink light.

✳ ✳ ✳

CHAPTER ONE

"Atta girl!" exclaimed Sophia Mendoza, as Mary Lou sailed over a fallen tree. The height of the jump would have sent shivers down the boots of some riders, but Sophia wasn't in the least bit afraid. How could anyone be scared when they were having fun with their best friend?

Mary Lou, Sophia's beautiful chestnut mare, whinnied with pleasure. She was enjoying this just as much as her rider! The horse galloped on, weaving through the woods, hooves thundering across the ground.

"This way," said Sophia, gently guiding

Mary Lou past some low branches. "Let's go!"

Sophia had loved Mary Lou ever since she could remember, and exploring was their favourite thing. Over the years living on the farm she called home, she had grown into a skilful rider, staying firm in the saddle despite the speed of Mary Lou's gallop. Sophia laughed as the wind whistled through her tawny brown hair. Around her neck she wore a crystal star pendant that glinted prettily as they sailed in and out of the trees.

When she was out in the wild, everything else disappeared. All she had to think about was the sunshine on her back, the reins in her hands and Mary Lou whisking her away on an adventure. Sophia urged her horse on, past shadowy glades and prickly thickets of brambles, until the afternoon sun began to fade and it was finally time to turn back. Together they galloped into a grassy meadow, towards a neat paddock surrounded by a tall wooden fence – home.

"Last jump," whispered Sophia, leaning over Mary Lou's neck. "Let's make it a good one!"

Mary Lou's ears went back as she pushed firmly off the ground, leaping over the fence with ease. She whinnied happily and slowed down to an easy trot.

"Perfect," laughed Sophia, slipping to the ground. She kissed the horse's nose, before adding, "As always!"

Mary Lou nickered, nudging Sophia tenderly. While the girl patted her neck and chattered to her, the horse noticed something out of the corner of her eye. What was that pink shimmer of light hovering above the farmhouse? Mary Lou blinked in surprise. But when she opened her eyes and looked again the light had disappeared.

Sophia hadn't noticed anything strange, she

was more troubled by how quickly the sun was starting to set. She took Mary Lou's reins and led her hurriedly across the paddock.

"It's getting late," she said. "We need to get you back to your stable before..."

"...Mum finds out?"

Sophia groaned. Her little brother, Marco, popped out from behind the stable block, beaming from ear to ear. He was only nine years old, but he had already learned some impressive detective skills.

"Mum is going to freak when she finds out you took Mary Lou out of the paddock!" he said.

Mary Lou and Sophia exchanged a secret nervous glance.

"I'm just guessing of course," Marco continued, "since I heard her say to you earlier, 'Don't even think about taking Mary Lou outside the paddock'."

Sophia gave him a playful punch in the ribs. She really didn't want to get caught breaking the rules, but it had been such a lovely, sunshiny afternoon. It almost felt wrong *not* to go out and have an adventure.

"Luckily Mum never has to find out," said Sophia, thinking fast. "She's busy making dinner, and you know how lasagne always gets the better of her."

To her surprise, Marco didn't reply. Instead his smile faded and his big brown eyes grew even wider than usual. Suddenly, Sophia was aware that someone was standing behind her.

"Hey Mum!" she gulped, spinning around.

Sophia's mum glared at her daughter. One hand was on her hip, the other was holding a pizza box.

"I didn't make dinner," she said firmly. "I ordered in."

Quick as a flash, Marco swept past his sister, lifted the box out of his mum's hand and made a dash for the house. "I'll just bring this inside. Bye!"

Sophia's tummy did a flip. Mary Lou bowed her head and looked down at the ground. They really were in trouble now.

"How many times have I told you that you're not allowed to go riding off the farm?" said Sophia's mum.

"Mary Lou needed to stretch her legs," argued Sophia. She sighed. Her mum had a way of looking at her that made it impossible not to tell the truth. "I just took her along the track," she added quietly. "Dad and I used to ride it all the time."

Her mum's eyes softened. She stepped forward to stroke Mary Lou, then led the horse towards the stable and started getting her ready for bed.

"I am just trying to keep you safe," she said gently.

"I'm a good rider," replied Sophia, fetching Mary Lou's water bucket. "You don't have to worry about me."

Her mum raised an eyebrow. "Really? Last week you rode out in a thunderstorm to catch a runaway chicken. The week before I caught you both playing tag with a bull."

"Fair point, Mum."

Sophia glanced over at Mary Lou, who now had her bridle removed and was busy enjoying a lovely neck rub. It wasn't that they *intended* to do dangerous things, they just sort of – happened.

"Why can't you ever do some safe, typical teenage stuff?" asked her mum. "You could make some friends, go to the movies, have sleepovers. It could be fun."

"Friends are overrated," said Sophia, giving

Mary Lou a goodnight cuddle. "I'm more of a rebellious loner with a love of adventure that can't help driving her mum nuts."

Sophia's mum shook her head and chuckled, leaning in to join the hug.

"You got that right," she agreed. "Oh, and about you sneaking out."

"Grounded?" said Sophia. "Yep. I thought so!"

Cock-a-doodle-dooooo!

The farm's big red cockerel was perched on the wall outside Sophia's bedroom. He fluffed up his feathers, took a deep breath and crowed again. *Cock-a-doodle-doo!* It was his job to wake everyone up bright and early each morning, and he was never late.

Sophia yawned sleepily, did a big stretch, then lifted up the window and popped her head out.

"And a very good morning to *you!*" she said,

giving the cockerel a friendly wave.

Sophia slid her feet into a pair of slippers and headed downstairs. She could already smell the warm, homey scent of her mum's pancakes cooking in the kitchen. On the landing she passed the photo of her dad, Miles Mendoza. Sophia and Marco still missed him so much – sometimes it was hard to remember that he wasn't just out in the stables feeding the horses or doing jobs around the farm. As she went past, Sophia gently kissed her fingers and pressed them to his picture frame, just as she did every single day.

"Morning, Dad," she whispered.

Sophia was still staring into her dad's kind face when the doorbell rang.

Ding-dong!

"I'll get it!" shouted Sophia, taking the stairs three at a time. She skidded up to the front door in seconds, but when she threw it open no one was there. Sophia stepped out onto the porch, looking left and right. "That's strange," she mumbled, before turning back inside and almost tripping over a shiny silver box sitting in the middle of the doormat.

Sophia gazed at the box. How had that got there? A shimmer of magenta light hovered behind her as she looked again for a delivery person. When she finally gave up and carried the box inside, the light darted away.

Sophia took the box in to show her mum and Marco. Although it was heavy and sturdy, the outside had been beautifully decorated with a pair of gold and lilac horses. Sophia gasped when she noticed her name engraved on the top.

"What is it?" asked Marco.

Sophia's mum watched anxiously as her daughter carefully lifted the lid. Inside the box was a smart invitation, written on sparkly card:

> ## WE ARE PLEASED TO INVITE YOU TO ATTEND
>
> # NUNCIOR ACADEMY
>
> ## THE WORLD'S LEADING SCHOOL FOR PROMISING EQUESTRIAN RIDERS

Sophia's face lit up. A school where she would get to ride all day? A place for her to be with horses as part of her lessons? It sounded like a dream come true! She looked at her mum, pleadingly. "Can I go?"

"And can I have her room?" chipped in Marco.

Sophia's mum frowned. "What about your school here?"

"They don't let me bring my *horse* to lessons!"

said Sophia, "and it's not like anyone would miss me there."

"But I would miss you," said her mum. "Marco would miss you."

Marco began to nod, then quickly shook his head. "Actually, the new bedroom *would* heal the pain..."

His mum shot him a fierce look. Marco saw his cue to make a speedy exit as Sophia picked a brochure out of the box filled with information about Nuncior Academy. It sounded amazing.

"I know you worry about me," she said to her mum, "but I have a feeling that I am meant to do this."

Sophia's mum stared at the brochure for the longest time. At last she looked up and said, "I am sorry. I don't think this is a good idea."

"Mum! Seriously?" Sophia clutched her crystal pendant and felt herself starting to cry. This was a riding academy. Her mum knew that caring for horses had always been her dream. And surely ruining someone's dreams couldn't be right? "Dad would want me to go!" she blurted out. "If *he* were here, he..."

Sophia's mum turned her head away. "Our family has lost enough," she said, simply. "I don't want you leaving, Sophia."

There was nothing more to say. Sobbing, Sophia ran back up to her bedroom and slammed the door.

CHAPTER TWO

Sophia stayed inside all day. To be grounded and *not* going to Nuncior Academy – it was too depressing for words. As she lay there on her bed surrounded by her posters, cushions and special things, Sophia couldn't imagine a time when she would ever feel happy again. Without her dearest dreams, the whole world had turned grey and sad. She reached up to the shelf and pulled down a chunky book with a worn pink cover – the Mendoza family photo album.

"I wish you were here, Dad," whispered Sophia, gazing fondly at the pages of neatly mounted pictures. There she was aged five, her dad holding the reins to steady a cute palomino pony so she could sit on its back. Sophia was seven in the next shot, riding alongside her dad on holiday. Another showed Miles Mendoza watching proudly as Sophia, aged nine, rode out beyond the paddock. Sophia, her dad and horses – they just belonged together.

Far off across the stables, a mare whinnied in the evening air. It sounded like Mary Lou.

Sophia's nose twitched. She put down the album, then leapt up and pulled back the curtains. Her friend was calling her.

"I won't be long," she decided, suddenly realising that grounded or not, she couldn't stay put a minute more. "I'll just run to the stables and check that Mary Lou is OK."

Taking care to be as quiet as a mouse, Sophia knotted one of her dad's old checked shirts around her middle to keep warm, then lifted up the window. Before you could say, "discover your destiny," she had stepped onto the ledge, inched along the roof and climbed down a drainpipe. She tore across the farmyard, panting excitedly, and slid into the stable.

Mary Lou was nibbling on some hay when Sophia appeared. She gave a soft neigh of surprise, then stepped forward to affectionately nuzzle Sophia's chest.

"I hope I didn't get you into trouble yesterday," said Sophia, stroking Mary Lou's soft, sandy mane. As she spoke the horse stood patiently, listening to every word. "Mum doesn't get how much we need to run sometimes. Remember our rides with Dad? He always said I was destined for something *extraordinary*. I just wish I knew what that was."

Outside, high above the stables, clusters of stars began to come out, glittering brilliantly in the velvety sky. Sophia turned her face up towards them, searching for an answer.

"Do you ever feel like there has to be more out there?" she wondered out loud. "Like there's more inside you that's bursting to come out?"

Mary Lou pawed the ground with her hoof. Without even thinking, Sophia leapt on her back and together they rode out into the night. They cantered across the paddock, towards the far fence with the meadow beyond.

"What should I do?" said Sophia, hesitating for a moment.

As if in reply, a dazzling shooting star streaked across the sky, lighting up the trees far ahead. Emboldened, Sophia spurred Mary Lou on. The horse leapt over the paddock fence and out across the grass. It was time to gallop free in the countryside, chasing stars!

It was late by the time Sophia slid back in through her bedroom window, breathless but exhilarated by the fresh night air. She put her feet down on the rug carefully, trying not to make a sound...

"Oh. Erm ... hi?"

Sophia's mum was sitting on her bed, looking right at her. The photo album was perched on her lap. She patted the duvet, inviting Sophia to come and sit down.

"You know I miss him, too," said Sophia's mum, smiling at a picture of the whole family together.

Sophia nodded, fiddling with her star pendant. "I can't believe that it's been five years."

"He'd love that you still wear the necklace he gave you," said her mum. "You were his shining star."

Sophia smiled, then pointed to another photo.

This one showed her dad in his check shirt, lifting little Sophia up into the air.

Mum chuckled. "He would have also got a kick out of you wearing his old shirt. Although..." she sniffed one of the sleeves and pulled a face, "it's definitely due for a wash!"

"When I was riding with Dad, it felt like I could do anything," said Sophia, grinning back at her. "Like the whole world was there in my reach."

"He loved you so much, Sophia," said her mum, looking at the album again. "He used to tell me that you were destined for something..."

Sophia and her mum said the words at the same time: "*Extraordinary.*"

"You remind me so much of him," said her mum. She looked at Sophia and smiled. "And you know that your dad *also* went to a riding academy."

Sophia's heart skipped a beat. "Really? Wait," she said, warily. "What do you mean, 'also'?"

Her mum kissed her on the forehead, then quietly got up to leave, eyes twinkling.

"I mean you better get some sleep. We've got a lot of packing to do tomorrow if you're going off to a new school."

Sophia gasped in surprise. Before her mum could say another word, she scrambled across the bedroom and gave her the biggest hug ever.

She, Sophia Mendoza, was going to be a student at Nuncior Academy. Maybe sometimes dreams really did come true!

* * *

CHAPTER
THREE

The next day was a flurry of writing lists, sorting out suitcases and packing. At first Sophia struggled to believe it was really happening, until it was finally time to load her things into the car and get on the road. After a long, teary goodbye with Mary Lou, and lots of promises from her mum and Marco to take the very best care of her, Sophia was ready to go.

Mum drove them to a pretty marina on the coast, a little way from home. At the end of the wooden jetty, Sophia spotted a small boat with a yellow sail bobbing gently in the water.

Neat, looping letters along its side read: *NUNCIOR ACADEMY*.

"That must be my lift!" she said.

"What?" spluttered Marco. "Your school bus is a *boat*? You are so lucky!"

Sophia's mum took her case out of the car and put it down at the end of the jetty.

"We're going to miss you," she whispered, wrapping her daughter up in her arms. "Make sure you call us. A lot!"

Sophia nodded hard, her eyes glistening with excited, happy tears. She bent down and squeezed Marco on the shoulders. "Now it's all on you to get into trouble while I'm gone."

Marco grinned. "I'll try my best, sis!"

Together, the family faced the sea. The little sailing boat glinted and sparkled merrily in the morning sun, inviting Sophia to come aboard. Her new adventure was about to begin!

Sophia pulled her dad's checked shirt a little tighter around her jeans, scooped up her case, then with a big smile and a wave turned and ran towards the boat.

"Hello!" she called, jumping down onto the deck, keen to see if there were any other students on board.

There was no one there.

Sophia went to the captain's cabin and opened the door. "Thanks for the lift," she said politely, "I'm Soph—"

Sophia's eyes widened. The cabin was completely empty, too. How was she going to travel to her new school alone? Suddenly, as if it could magically read her thoughts, the boat revved into life. Sophia watched her mum and Marco get smaller and smaller as the vessel began to glide swiftly out across the sea.

"I've heard of driverless cars," murmured

Sophia, "but driverless boats? This academy *is* fancy!"

She sat down and breathed in the salty air. All she had to do now was enjoy the journey. With the morning wind dancing in her hair and the sun glinting on the water, the ocean had never looked more beautiful.

"Not a bad way to get to school," she decided, as the waves tumbled by.

But just when the last sight of land had disappeared behind her, the boat began to rumble and shake. Sophia, knocked from her seat, gripped onto the side of the boat with her hands and peered over the edge. Something was happening – something so *extraordinary* she almost couldn't believe her own eyes!

The boat began to glitter with diamond-bright light. Then, to Sophia's amazement, two shimmering fairy wings appeared, one on either side of the boat! Each was covered with rows of white feathers that moved gently up and down. Sophia, her luggage and the entire boat was lifted out of the sea and up into the sky. Within moments, they were high above candyfloss clouds, gliding towards a mist-draped faraway land.

Sophia felt a fizz of excitement rushing inside her chest. "What kind of school is this?" she whispered out loud.

Without warning, the magical mists cleared and the boat began to dive back down again, floating effortlessly towards the lush island below. As it got closer, Sophia could spot rainbow-coloured sandy beaches surrounded by a sapphire sea; icy, snow-capped mountains and lush green treetops speckled with flowers. It was the most beautiful place she had ever seen.

"OK," she reasoned. "You fell asleep and this

is just a dream."

But if it was a dream, she wasn't the only one dreaming. Sophia looked up to see more fairy boats riding through the sky, to the left and right of her own. Each one carried a student – girls and boys about the same age as her. Some leapt up and waved, some called out an excited "Hello", whilst others were simply gazing, entranced, at the island below.

Sophia waited as her fairy boat landed smoothly in the water, taking in every spectacular detail. More boats were touching down all around her, docking along the edge of a magnificent emerald pond.

"What a delightfully dreamy day!" exclaimed a voice.

Sophia, who had just been looking down at her pendant, lifted her head with a start. A small creature with a pink snout and lilac fur was waiting to greet her at the side of the boat, beaming from ear to ear. Although he couldn't have been taller than her knee, Sophia noticed that he was dressed in a smart groom's uniform, richly trimmed in purple and gold.

The creature beckoned towards the shore. "Did you have a pleasant trip?" he asked brightly, as if arriving by fairy boat was the most normal thing in the world.

"It was great, thank you," replied Sophia. "May I just ask ... where am I? Who are you?"

The little creature didn't have any time for questions. Instead he pulled his pocket watch out of his jacket and tutted. "The tock is ticking! If you would please follow me." He picked up Sophia's suitcase and marched away, leaving her to hurry after.

"Hey!" shouted Sophia, trying to catch his arm. "At least tell me who you are?"

The creature paused. "I'm Fernakus," he said. "Hello and welcome. We Dwerpins have been working at the academy for generations."

"*Dwerpins*?" said Sophia.

Fernakus nodded briskly, but kept on walking. Bewildered, Sophia followed, trying not to stumble as she spotted more little Dwerpins bustling around students, carrying cases, swapping instructions and hurrying new arrivals along a beautiful marble colonnade draped in tropical flowers.

"Mind the Flutterbunnies," said Fernakus, as they passed underneath a canopy of green trees. Sophia gasped as a fluffy yellow rabbit with butterfly wings popped out from amongst the leaves, before fluttering happily over their heads.

There was too much to take in. Sophia had expected to be going to a riding academy – a place filled with horses and stables, not flying boats and magical bunny rabbits. Perhaps there had been a mistake? She pulled her invitation out to show Fernakus. This time when she read it however, the letters in *NUNCIOR* had magically rearranged themselves:

WE ARE PLEASED TO INVITE YOU TO ATTEND

UNICORN ACADEMY

THE WORLD'S LEADING SCHOOL FOR PROMISING EQUESTRIAN RIDERS

"Unicorns?" Sophia repeated, stunned.

"Oh I see," said Fernakus, tutting as the crowds of students swelled around them. "You're one of those goof-maloofs who grew up believing that there's no such thing as magic. That unicorns aren't real."

"Because they're not!" Sophia flashed back.

Fernakus lowered his voice and moved a little closer. "Don't fret, you've come to the most wonderful place in the world. We keep this place secret, but magic is as real as you and me. This is Unicorn Island and it's the source of it *all*." And with that he took her case and joined the long line of Dwerpins sweeping off with towering piles of luggage. "Now you toodle along," he called, "and I'll take your case up to your room!"

Sophia spun around to watch him go, and for the very first time took in the view ahead of her. A vast fairy-tale castle rose up towards the sky, white marble towers gleaming with such brilliance it almost took her breath away. There were turquoise-topped domes and turrets, elegant bridges, crystal glass windows and blossom trailing over the walkways.

"Gangway!" shouted a Dwerpin, struggling to push a rack full of fancy clothes. The rail was so loaded the poor little creature couldn't see where he was going, accidentally knocking Sophia to the ground.

"Hey!"

The Dwerpin was full of apologies, but the owner of the clothes strutted past without even stopping to see if she was all right. Sophia checked out the girl's glossy red hair, expensive clothes and nose held high in the air. She wouldn't forget her in a hurry.

As soon as the stranger had swooshed by, a hand reached down and helped Sophia back up to her feet.

"Hi, I'm Ava!" said a girl with a sweet, open face and pink pigtails. "It's so nice to meet you!"

Ava pulled Sophia into a tight hug, making her blush with shyness.

"Hi, Ava," mumbled Sophia. "What is this place? I came here to ride horses."

"Ah, so you're not a *legacy* student, then?" said Ava, nodding kindly. "My brothers went here, and when I got my invitation, they secretly told me everything. You must be totally confused and weirded out!"

Sophia smiled. "Just a little," she admitted.

Ava took Sophia's hand and quickly led her up the marble steps towards a magnificent courtyard in front of the entrance to the academy. In the centre, there was a sculpture of three noble unicorns rearing up on their hind legs. Each statue was so exquisitely carved Sophia could almost believe she was looking up at real animals, but then a bell chimed and something even more incredible appeared.

UNICORN ACADEMY

Sophia gasped in surprise as five colourful unicorns pranced majestically out into the courtyard, each ridden by a teacher dressed in an academy uniform. The unicorns gazed regally down at the students before them, their tails and manes shimmering with magical sparkles.

"Those are unicorns..." she told Ava in an astonished whisper, "...real unicorns."

* * ✶

CHAPTER FOUR

Sophia had to pinch herself to be quite sure she was awake. Her eyes, as big as saucers, moved from left to right, trying to absorb every detail. Each of the unicorns standing before her was striking in a unique and different way, with its own gorgeous mane of colours. She stood, spellbound, as an impressive unicorn with golden hooves and a tumbling golden mane stepped forward. Her rider was a lady with grey hair and kind eyes, dressed smartly in jodhpurs and a navy velvet jacket.

"Welcome to Unicorn Academy!" she

announced in a clear voice. "I'm Ms Primrose, your new headteacher. Before we begin, I think we should make the place look a bit more festive on such an important day. Don't you agree, Ethera?"

The unicorn she was sitting on gracefully stretched out one leg and knelt the other on the ground, then swooped her horn up to the academy turrets with a grand flourish. The students cried out in surprise as a fountain of glittery magic sprinkled in all directions. Wherever the magic touched, a colourful decoration appeared. Within moments the academy was bedecked with twinkly bunting, spiralling streamers and long, billowing banners.

"Ava," said Sophia. "This is unreal!"

Once she was satisfied with Ethera's work, Ms Primrose began her speech. "This is Unicorn Island. All of the world's magic comes from here. And unicorns are its protectors – the only creatures mighty enough to keep the island safe from danger." She paused to study the hushed crowd of young students before she continued, "You have all been invited to join a long history of Unicorn Riders..."

A ripple of excitement spread through the crowd.

"This was definitely not the kind of riding academy I expected," murmured Sophia.

"Some of you have been chosen for your extraordinary skills and talents," explained Ms Primrose. "Others follow in the footsteps of a family member who was a Unicorn Rider before you."

Ava nudged her new friend in the ribs, pointing across to a student standing on the opposite side of the courtyard. Sophia recognised the red-haired girl who had walked past her earlier without bothering to help her up. As she stood there smirking confidently, Sophia couldn't help feeling a little envious. The girl was clearly a legacy student, while she was still such a newbie.

Ms Primrose extended her arms to include everyone standing before her. "*All* of you have the potential to bond with a unicorn, and when you do, it will unlock the unicorn's powerful magic."

As if on cue, Ethera's gilded hooves began to glow. She stamped her feet and fireworks burst in the air around her, exploding starbursts of colour that made the students clap and cheer with delight.

"I look forward to seeing you make the most of this wonderful opportunity," Ms Primrose said sincerely, "but for now please get settled. Unicorn matching begins at dawn."

The pupils hurried eagerly into the academy

building, keen to explore and make friends.

"Let me get this straight," said Sophia, as she and Ava trailed after the others, "We're going to learn how to ride unicorns and protect magic for the entire world?"

"Yep!" Ava beamed joyfully, dimples appearing in each cheek.

Sophia nodded thoughtfully. She had been yearning for adventure, but this was off the charts!

The students followed the teaching staff into the atrium, a lofty glass dome supported by sleek marble columns. Crystal archways at the top refracted the sunlight beautifully, creating rainbows that turned slowly throughout the day. Ava pointed at a pair of lifts in the centre being raised and lowered on magical lotus vines.

"This is even more incredible than my brothers

said it would be," she gushed.

A rather severe-looking teacher on a silver unicorn clapped her hands to get everyone's attention. "New students gather here!" she announced in a clipped voice. "It's time for your rooms to be allocated."

Sophia stepped forward, keen to hear more, slotting in beside a boy with tousled black hair and a cheeky grin who was noisily taking selfies on his smart phone.

"That's it, work the hair!" he cooed to himself, "Hashtag: *Rory's dream life!*"

Sophia and Ava couldn't help but laugh.

"Rory – that's me," the boy smiled, pleased to have an audience.

BAMPF!

There was a blinding burst of light and the silver unicorn suddenly appeared behind Rory, giving him such a fright he tossed his phone up into the air. The strict teacher reached out a hand and caught it firmly in her grip.

"We take our oath of secrecy very seriously here, Mr Carmichael," she said. She slid the smart phone into her jacket pocket as she turned and rode away.

"Oh well," said Rory, with a happy-go-lucky shrug.

He was about to plead to get his phone back, when the girl with the glossy red hair interrupted him, cutting to the front of the dorm queue as if she was royalty.

"Who is she?" asked Sophia.

"That's Valentina Furi," replied Ava. "She's a super-legacy. Her relatives were some of the original founders of the Unicorn Academy. Her aunt is Ms Furi, the one who confiscated Rory's phone. She's the magic teacher."

Sophia watched the girl smile up at

Ms Furi, who, once she was fairly certain no other students were looking, discreetly smiled back. So Valentina was basically Unicorn Academy royalty – how frustrating. Sophia resolved to stay out of her way for as long as she possibly could.

When the last new student had taken their place in the atrium, Ms Furi and her unicorn, Ghost, were ready to begin. Sophia listened carefully to the instructions, then watched in wonder as sparkles of colour began to pop above their heads. The sparkles fizzed and clustered, gradually forming themselves into bright, glowing gemstones. The atrium soon filled with deep red rubies, green emeralds and glinting purple amethysts. Sophia looked at Ava and Rory. All three of them had a blue sapphire floating in the air above them.

"Look!" cried Ava, seeing it, too. "We're going to be in Sapphire dorm! It's fate! I just know we're going to be besties, Sophia!"

Sophia blushed, then hastily followed Rory up to the stained-glass doors that led the way to their dormitory.

Sophia, Ava and Rory found themselves in a light and airy common room with a stunning aquamarine chandelier glinting in the centre. There were doorways leading off to the bedrooms and bathrooms, and a curving spiral staircase inlaid with marble and gold. Despite the beauty of the chamber, everything was cosy and comfortable. Sophia instantly felt at home.

"Nice!" said Rory, nodding his approval.

"There are unicorn decorations everywhere!" marvelled Ava. "Did someone read my diary?"

Sophia's heart sank as she spotted Valentina Furi come into the dormitory.

"Great," Valentina sniffed, glaring at the Sapphire dorm students. "This is going to be fun."

She stalked off to her room, as the last two Sapphire students appeared – Layla and Isabel. Layla stumbled in loaded down with books and writing equipment, which she promptly spilled all over the carpet.

"Hello," she said gratefully, as Sophia and Ava helped her pick everything up again. "I knew something was up when I got an invitation to a riding academy. I have never been on a horse in my life! I had a hunch this was some sort of elite, secret school."

"Layla? I think I'm your roomie!" shouted Isabel, a sporty blonde girl dressed in shorts and trainers. "Want some help carrying your stuff?" she said, plucking Layla's books out of her arms. "I'm very strong!"

"Let's all go find our spaces!" said Rory, once they'd exchanged hellos. "Sophia and Ava – the last door on the left has got your names on it."

Sophia ran along the corridor and peeped into the bedroom at the end. Inside was the most amazing, magical space she could ever have imagined. Each side of the room had been decorated to match the student's personality. Ava's side had pretty green creepers curling in a canopy over the sleeping area and lamps shaped like tulip petals.

"I love, love, *love* it!" she cried, blissfully falling backwards onto the bedspread.

Sophia's side was lit by twinkly pointed stars. There were the softest blankets, fleecy cushions, and a cosy chair for her to snuggle up in. Her eyes smiled with pleasure when she spotted the string of family photos pinned up above her bed.

At the far end of the room, there was a pair of tall glass windows with a spectacular view across the academy grounds. Sophia pushed the windows open and stepped out onto the balcony just as the first stars were coming out to meet the evening sky.

"This is perfect," she said quietly, gazing up at them. "Dad, I think I found my extraordinary."

✴ ✴ ✴

CHAPTER
FIVE

Later, as she unpacked, Sophia heard lots of commotion outside and rushed to join Ava on the balcony.

"Look," whispered Ava, pointing down one at of the bridges arching over the academy moat. "Someone's been messing around that statue."

Sophia followed the direction of Ava's outstretched finger, then raised her eyebrows in surprise. The unicorn statue at the far end of the bridge had been dressed in a pair of over-sized boxer shorts! The shorts were baggy and brightly-patterned, and clearly did not belong.

Sophia's surprise quickly turned to amusement. "Brilliant!" she chuckled.

"Looks like we've got a joker in our class," Ava agreed.

Hooves click-clacked on the cobbles, and Ms Furi suddenly trotted out on Ghost. Even from all those floors above, the girls could tell she was furious.

"Whichever student is responsible for this," Ms Furi bellowed up at the dormitories, "*will* face consequences!"

Sophia and Ava shrunk back from the balcony railings, not wanting to attract the teacher's fierce stare. As they stole inside, Sophia noticed a bush rustling suspiciously in the academy gardens. She squeezed Ava's arm. The culprit was still down there, just metres away from Ms Furi. A familiar mop of black hair suddenly popped out of the undergrowth. Rory! Quick as a flash, their dorm buddy looked up, shot them both a mischievous wink, then ducked back out of sight.

Sophia couldn't help but giggle ... until she heard the growling.

Grrr! Grrrr! Grrrrrr!

"What now?" spluttered Ava, turning pale in fright.

Sophia listened. Someone or something nearby was making a horrible, snarling sound. She listened again. "It's coming from inside our dorm."

Ava was jittery with nerves, but Sophia took charge. Together, they tiptoed back through the Sapphire common room and up to the second-floor landing.

GRRR! GRRRR! GRRRRRR!

The noise was getting louder, and it didn't sound any more friendly. The closer they got to

Layla and Isabel's bedroom, the worse it got. Sophia put on a brave face. She had to look in there to check the girls were safe and not being gobbled up by some sort of magical monster. Before Ava could try to change her mind, she clasped the handle and flung open the door...

Layla looked up from her chair. She had a purple book laid open on her lap, covered with intricate pictures and writing. A blue beast with lizard eyes and pointy teeth jumped up and down in the air magically above the pages, roaring fiercely. The Frost Goblin! As soon as Layla saw the other students, she shut the book and the beast instantly disappeared.

"Sorry," she said. "I was just looking in my new book."

"But that little critter," stuttered Sophia, "he was nasty! And making enough noise to wake up the whole dorm..."

"Maybe not the *whole* dorm," chipped in Ava, pointing to the bed in the corner where Isabel was still fast asleep.

"The Frost Goblin wasn't real," Layla explained, pushing her glasses up her nose. "He was a vision from the Sparklebook. I found it on my bookshelf. It's an encyclopaedia all about Unicorn Island and it's *definitely* enchanted."

She brought the book out into the common room so Sophia and Ava could take a proper look. As the three girls sat cross-legged in front of the fireplace, the Sparklebook gave off a soft, purple light. The cover was inlaid with mysterious symbols and crescent moons, and there was a star-encrusted unicorn in the centre. Layla carefully turned the gilt-edged pages and Sophia breathed in the aroma of old parchment and forgotten libraries.

"I'm in love with it already," gushed Layla. "Look at the pictures!"

Ava and Sophia watched in hushed silence as each illustration lifted magically off the page, glowing in the air before them. Unicorns cantered, clouds moved and Flutterbunnies buzzed amongst the flowers. They could smell, see and hear everything.

"Wow," gasped Ava. "But why spend so long looking at Frost Goblins?"

"As we are training to be Unicorn Island heroes, I thought I should also read about some of the villains," replied Layla.

Sophia sat up. "So this place isn't all lollipops and rainbows?"

Layla shook her head. She opened a new section of the book and more Frost Goblins snapped and snarled at them, followed by mysterious forms called Swampshifters and a giant one-eyed monster known as a Silver Mountain Cyclops.

"They come from the island kingdom of Grimoria," said Layla. "Home base of something called 'Grim Magic'." She turned the page and a new image appeared. This time a tall, thin woman with long, pointy fingers magically rose up. This magical woman was taller than your average grown-up and her fierce features and the sly gleam in her eye made each girl instantly recoil in alarm.

"Who is that?" muttered Sophia, taking in the woman's coal-coloured crown.

"Ravenzella," answered Layla. "Queen of Grimoria." She turned back the page, revealing an image of the queen rising out of swirling darkness to do battle with a figure seated on a unicorn. "She almost took over Unicorn Island, but a brave Unicorn Rider defeated her and

55

locked her away in the Cell of Eternity, making Grimoria vanish."

She closed the book and stared earnestly at her dorm buddies.

"Time for bed I think," said Ava in a quiet voice.

As the last light went out in the Unicorn Academy, the shimmer of a magical jet-black creature whispered to a shadowy figure outside the dormitories. Then the shimmery black creature rose up into the sky and vanished into the night. Only when it arrived in a far-off crystal cave did it dare to reveal itself. An enormous ogre prowling the lonely cave tunnels snorted in surprise as the blackness suddenly transformed into a Shadow Sprite, buzzing restlessly just above his head.

"Ooh! Lighty-bug!" grunted the ogre, lunging at the creature.

"Stop it, Ash," snapped the sprite, effortlessly ducking out of his reach. "It's me, Crimsette! I've got a message for our queen."

The ogre put his fist down and stared nervously along the tunnel. At the very end was the source of his fear – a glistening pale-blue cage made of steely gem crystals. A dark figure lurked inside this prison. Crimsette flew as close as she dared.

"It is time, Ravenzella."

The figure smiled a horrible, twisted smile.

"Well, well," she sneered. "How lovely..."

* * *

CHAPTER SIX

Everyone in Sapphire dorm was up long before the sunrise. It was unicorn matching day and the students couldn't think or talk about anything else. They had been told to gather at the edge of Wonderwood Forest straight after breakfast. As she walked over to the meeting point with her new friends, Sophia felt a tingle of excitement. The idea of getting to know a real-life unicorn really was a dream come true. She thought fondly of Mary Lou and the special connection that they shared. Nothing could ever replace her in Sophia's heart – they would always be friends forever – but she couldn't wait to go riding again.

"I feel super-nervous and a little scared," said Ava, "yet I can't stop smiling."

Layla nodded energetically. "I've never done gymnastics, but my stomach is doing some serious somersaults!"

"Try and shake it out," Sophia said, helpfully, showing her how to jump up and down on the spot and wiggle her hands. "If unicorns are anything like horses, you don't want them to see you scared."

Layla's face fell. "Really? Now I'm even *more* nervous!"

Sophia gave Layla an encouraging smile as they stepped aside to let Ms Primrose ride past on Ethera. The unicorn looked even more splendid today than the first time they had seen her, gold hooves trotting so elegantly and head perfectly poised in a deep curve. When they arrived by the thick line of trees at the edge of the forest, Ms Furi was waiting on Ghost. She called everyone to attention – it was time for the matching to begin.

"Good morning, students!" announced Ms Primrose. "This is the place where the unicorns of this island roam. Today you will each discover if one of those unicorns is destined to become yours."

Ms Furi quietly reached forward to tickle Ghost's ears. Although the teacher's face was as serious as usual, Sophia could tell how much she loved her unicorn. Ghost's long eyelashes fluttered happily, enjoying the fuss, and she gave a little whinny of pleasure.

As the headteacher continued with her instructions, tiny dots of light began to emerge out of the forest shadows. Orange, blue, yellow, green – every colour of the rainbow was there.

A dot darted by and Sophia was stunned to discover that each light was actually a tiny fairy, no bigger than her finger.

"Right on time!" said Ms Primrose. "The Fate Fairies are some of the most ancient residents of this island. If you find the unicorn that is your destined match, your Fate Fairy will glow more brightly."

The students glanced nervously across at each other as the Fate Fairies sought them out. Sophia watched spellbound as a deep pink fairy with dancing eyes fluttered out of the trees and hovered close beside her shoulder.

Ms Primrose explained that every student who matched with a unicorn would be presented with their uniforms at the Enchanted Archway later that afternoon.

"For those who *don't*," added Ms Furi, "becoming a Unicorn Rider is not your destiny.

You will be sent home."

Several students shuddered anxiously. Only Valentina was wearing a smug grin, making out that she didn't have a care in the world. Sophia felt more determined than ever to find a unicorn. She had to prove to the world, and Valentina, that she deserved to be here!

"Just follow your heart and see if it leads you to a unicorn," Ms Primrose advised. "And remember that parts of this island, such as the Crystal Caves, are forbidden to students. There's only one strict rule – as you search, do not go beyond the Shimmerstone Wall."

Everyone nodded, eager to get on their way.

Ethera's horn lit up and an emerald firework soared up towards to the sky.

"Your destiny awaits," declared Ms Primrose. "Good luck!"

Isabel led the way into the forest at a sprint, with the rest of the students fanning out behind her. Sophia, Ava and Layla picked a mossy path lined with ferns and frothy, bell-shaped blossoms. Three little Fate Fairies floated along beside them.

"It's ... it's like a *dream*," gasped Sophia. She had never explored anywhere quite so beautiful. The colours, the beautiful flower perfumes, the Fate Fairies – all of her senses felt alive.

Ava sighed with happiness. "Just when I thought this place couldn't get any better!"

"It's just unbelievable," said Layla. "I wonder where the unicorns ... *argggh*!"

A strong and powerful ice-white unicorn burst its way through the ferns and came pounding along the path towards them. Sophia and Ava leapt out of the way in the nick of time, but Layla was knocked off balance and fell sprawling to the ground. The towering creature raised itself onto its hind legs and snorted proudly before her.

Layla straightened her glasses, then dared herself to look back. Why was this headstrong animal standing next to her? Everyone knew she couldn't even ride.

"Your Fate Fairy!" whispered Sophia, pointing into the air beside Layla. "It's glowing!"

Sophia was right. The orb around Layla's Fate Fairy was glowing a rich, golden yellow. This had to be her unicorn!

"Hello," Layla said shyly, scrambling to her feet. "It looks like we're a team."

"Congratulations!" gushed Ava.

Isabel ran back down the track and skidded to a halt beside them. She'd heard the commotion and assumed that such a powerful unicorn had to be searching for a sporty girl like her.

"She can't be yours, Layla," Isabel insisted.

"There's got to have been a mistake. If *that's* not my unicorn, who could be?"

Suddenly, a sing-song neighing echoed through the forest. Another unicorn!

"This way!" said Sophia.

The girls hurried down the track, following the sound. A little further long, a stunning electric-blue unicorn was standing in a clearing, drinking cool water from a stream. Sophia thought it was very handsome with its eye-catching pink and blue mane, but when the unicorn spotted the students, the poor thing became so frightened it hid, trembling, behind a tree.

Isabel sighed. Her Fate Fairy was glowing.

"He can't be *mine*, can he?" she asked. "Really?"

Ava and Sophia shrugged, leaving Isabel, Layla and their unicorn matches to make their way back to the academy.

"Come on," said Ava, linking arms with Sophia. "Let's keep wandering."

As they walked deeper and deeper into the forest, Sophia wondered if she would ever find her match. Every couple of minutes there was a shout as someone else met the unicorn destined to be their companion on the island. Rory soon passed them with a mischievous purple unicorn, closely followed by Valentina.

"You've both still had no luck?" she said smugly, shooting a mocking look at her own unicorn companion. "Oh dear."

Sophia felt a pang of envy as she watched the fiery-orange creature stepping alongside Valentina. The unicorn looked beautiful but haughty, just like the young Ms Furi.

Ava tried to take Sophia's mind off things by leading her into a glade filled with tiger lilies. These weren't just any ordinary tiger lilies though;

they were magical. The stripy flowers swayed from side to side in the breeze, their tiger faces roaring happily in the sunshine.

"Aren't these just amazing?" Ava asked, kneeling down to smell their sweet perfume.

"Ava!" gasped Sophia. "Watch out!"

A majestic yellow unicorn pushed her face through the flowers and licked Ava on the nose! The creature leapt to her feet and danced around the girl, swishing her tail in delight.

Ava clapped her hands together, taking in the unicorn's gentle eyes and beautiful violet and turquoise mane. She was perfect in every way.

"I daren't look at my Fate Fairy," she cried. "Please be glowing ... please be glowing..."

Ting!

Ava's fairy shone star-bright. She really had met her unicorn match! Sophia smiled to congratulate the pair.

"We'll see you on the other side, OK?" said Ava.

Sophia nodded, waving bravely until Ava and her unicorn had disappeared down the path back to school. The second they had gone, her heart sank.

"Everyone has found their match apart from me," she said glumly.

Sophia was alone. Inside, she felt worried and a little scared that her time at the academy could be over already, until she lifted her hand up to her neck and felt the precious crystal in her star pendant.

"You can find a unicorn, Sophia," she told herself out loud. "You just need a better view."

Her eyes settled upon an ancient tree towering up ahead. It had magnificent, tangled branches, burnished gold leaves and a massive, twisted trunk like a spiral staircase. It would have been perfect for climbing, if it wasn't growing just beyond a wall built from gleaming blocks of stone.

"I'm guessing this is the Shimmerstone Wall," said Sophia, catching the eye of her Fate Fairy. "Ms Primrose said not to cross it, but this is a unicorn-finding emergency."

She checked the coast was clear, then straddled the wall in a single jump. "And if I'm going to be fighting evil, I think I can handle a quick trip out of bounds."

Sophia's Fate Fairy crossed her little arms and frowned, then dutifully followed after her.

"Oh!" gasped Sophia, clambering onto the tree. "Maybe this isn't so good..."

The ancient plant was twisting underneath her, its branches curling, pulling, tugging. Sophia found herself being carried into the heart of the tree, and suddenly realised that she was trapped.

Thwack!

A golden unicorn horn lunged at the branches, shocking the tree so that it instantly released its grip on Sophia. She fell back down to the forest floor, landing on the right side of the wall in an ungraceful heap.

"Oh my..."

Sophia looked up in awe. A spectacular opal-white unicorn was standing above her, lit by the sun shining through the trees. Her mane and tail were peppered with rainbow shades and her coat seemed to shimmer in the sunshine. She was the most stunning creature Sophia had ever seen.

"I did it!" she spluttered. "I found my unicorn!"

Her heart gave a joyful leap as she glanced across at her Fate Fairy and saw that it was glowing a deep shade of pink.

Only the unicorn seemed unimpressed. She turned on her hooves and began to walk back off into the woods.

"Wait!" begged Sophia. "You're my match! I have a feeling that I am supposed to be a Unicorn Rider."

The creature kept walking, her tail swishing impatiently with each step.

"Maybe you just need to get to know me?" said Sophia. "My name is Sophia. *Sophia Mendoza.*"

The unicorn stopped at once. While Sophia rattled on with her introductions about home, Mary Lou and her invitation to unicorn school, the creature's eyes became soft. She trotted back up the path and sniffed at Sophia's dad's check shirt, then nuzzled the girl gently with her nose. Finally she tossed her head and neighed, as if to say: "*It's a match!*"

Sophia felt a warm rush of happiness.

"So we're doing this?" she gasped, stroking the creature's neck. "Let's go!"

CHAPTER
SEVEN

Two by two, the students and their unicorns emerged from Wonderwood Forest. Valentina and her flame-coloured unicorn were the first back, but Ava, Layla, Isabel and Rory were only seconds behind. No one had seen Sophia. Ms Furi checked her pocket watch impatiently – it was nearly time to go inside.

Valentina raised an eyebrow at Ava and Layla. "It looks like your friend didn't find a unicorn. Oh well, that really is *too bad*."

"Cheer up, Val," chirped a voice. "I'm not leaving yet."

SOPHIA'S INVITATION

Ava and Layla shrieked with happiness. Sophia was running towards the group, followed by her rainbow-maned unicorn. Valentina scowled.

Ms Furi greeted the late arrivals with a beady stare. Then she reached over and pulled a single leaf out of the girl's hair. "Do you care to explain *this*, Ms Mendoza?"

Sophia looked confused. "What is...?"

"It's a leaf from a Tangletwist Tree," snapped Ms Furi. "You were specifically given instructions *not* to cross the Shimmerstone Wall."

"But I—"

Ava shot an anxious look at her friend.

"Breaking rules might be 'your thing' back home, Ms Mendoza, but we take this very seriously at Unicorn Academy." Ms Furi's face was now pale with anger. "I'm afraid this is grounds for dismissal."

Sophia heard the words, but she couldn't

quite believe them.

"This can't be happening," she whispered. "I'm sorry."

Ms Furi's voice remained firm. "Please head back to your dorm and pack your things."

"No!" blurted out Ava, clutching onto Layla's arm.

Crushed, Sophia gave her unicorn one last stroke, then turned and slowly trudged away.

Sophia had never felt so lonely. As she walked miserably up the steps to the academy courtyard, her heart grew heavier and heavier. She hadn't just let herself down, she had let her family down, too. She wondered how she would find the words to tell her mum that she had been expelled from school.

"What was I thinking?" she said sadly, walking past the gleaming marble statues dedicated to the Unicorn Academy's greatest heroes. "How could I ever become a Unicorn Rider?"

Sophia looked down at her ripped jeans and her beloved check shirt, still strewn with twigs and leaves from her struggle in the Tangletwist Tree. She didn't look anything like a hero. Compared to the honourable riders celebrated in the monuments around her, she—

Sophia stopped in front of a statue of a handsome, bearded man gazing out towards the ocean.

"Wait a minute," she murmured. "Is that my *dad*?"

"It is indeed."

Sophia spun on her heel and came face-to-face with Ms Primrose.

"I don't understand," said Sophia. "Was my dad a ... Unicorn Rider?"

Ms Primrose gave a little nod. "One of

our best."

"Why didn't he ever tell me?" asked Sophia. "I thought he was a lorry driver."

"He wasn't allowed to tell you," Ms Primrose told her softly, "but he told *us* all about you. Come with me."

The headteacher guided Sophia into the beautiful front lobby of the academy. They walked slowly, taking their time to study the display of photographs, certificates and artefacts mounted on pedestals.

"This is where we remember Unicorn Academy's proud history," explained Ms Primrose.

"There's my dad again!" exclaimed Sophia, pointing at a black and white class photo. "I knew he went to a riding school, but I wasn't expecting *this*."

"Like all Unicorn Riders, your father graduated

and became a protector of Unicorn Island. He left to raise your family back home, but always returned when we needed him," said Ms Primrose. She paused for a moment, before adding, "Five years ago, when the island was in the gravest of danger he came back to join the fight against Ravenzella."

"The Queen of Grimoria?" gasped Sophia.

"Yes," said Ms Primrose. "Your father sacrificed himself to save this island, and lock Ravenzella in the Cell of Eternity."

Sophia felt overwhelmed. "That was *him* in the Sparklebook? We always thought he died in an accident."

Ms Primrose put her arm around Sophia, then patiently explained how incredibly brave her father had been. It was a lot to take in. Sophia felt tears welling up in her eyes. On the same day that she had discovered this news, she would be leaving – returning to a life without magic and unicorns!

"You did break a rule today," Ms Primrose said carefully, pointing up to another photograph of Miles Mendoza riding his unicorn. "But I think you deserve another chance. I have faith that you will be more mindful of our rules moving forward."

"Thank you so much!" spluttered Sophia. "Hey! The unicorn that I matched with in the forest..."

"Yes," said Ms Primrose. "She was your father's unicorn. Her name is Wildstar."

Sophia repeated the name – *Wildstar*. It had a lovely feel to it.

The soft clip-clop of hooves echoed through the atrium lobby. Wildstar appeared, standing in the entrance to the building.

"You knew my dad?" whispered Sophia, reaching out her hand.

Wildstar whinnied gently, then wandered up

to the girl's side. The unicorn gazed sadly up at the pictures on the wall. She missed Sophia's dad, too.

"Unfortunately, when a unicorn loses her rider," said Ms Primrose, "they also lose their magical abilities."

"Oh!"

Poor Wildstar. Losing her magic as well as her best friend – it was almost too sad to think about. Sophia wished that she could find a way to help the unicorn...

"Ms Primrose!" she suddenly cried out. "Could it be up to *me* to bring her magic back?"

The headteacher's eyes twinkled mysteriously.

"Fate works in interesting ways, Sophia."

A little later, the new students and their unicorns began to trickle up to the Enchanted Archway, in the heart of the academy's perfectly manicured gardens. Ms Furi had told everyone to arrive by two o'clock and nobody dared to be late. Ava paced up and down, desperately looking out for a sign of Sophia. Her face lit up when she saw her friend making her way to join the group.

"Please, please, please tell me you can stay," she begged, taking both of Sophia's hands and squeezing them tightly.

Sophia grinned up at Wildstar, then nodded her head.

"Yay!" cheered Ava.

Ms Furi walked over and glared at Sophia, until Ms Primrose arrived and whispered something in her ear. A flash of disappointment passed across Ms Furi's face, and then she stalked away.

Ms Primrose turned to the assembled group.

"You have taken the next step towards becoming Unicorn Riders," she said in her clear, singsong voice. "The Fate Fairies will now name your unicorns and give out your riding uniforms."

As the Fate Fairies gathered into a shimmering cloud and began to flutter around the Enchanted Archway, Sophia wondered what her uniform might look like. The older students she'd seen around the academy always appeared very smartly dressed, mostly wearing crisp jodhpurs and glossy riding boots. Compared to them, she couldn't help but feel a little unsure of herself in her ripped jeans and old high-tops. What would her magical makeover be?

The little coloured orbs of light surrounding the Fate Fairies began to flare brightly. In unison, they summoned each rider and unicorn pairing:

"Ava and ... Leaf!"

As Ava stepped forward, the archway glowed with powerful fairy magic. Suddenly her everyday outfit was transformed into a beautiful forest-green tunic decorated with petals and butterflies.

Sophia clapped in approval. This wasn't like any school uniform she had ever seen before, but it was charming, sweet and one hundred per cent Ava.

"Look at you, Leaf!" marvelled Ava, embracing her unicorn. "Your saddle matches my dress."

The next hour was full of smiles and surprises, as each of the students were introduced in turn. Layla and her unicorn, Glacier, looked amazing in icy blues, pinks and snowflake whites. Rory was super-chuffed when the Fate Fairies dressed him and his unicorn, Storm, in vivid lightning flashes. Isabel's match, River, was still a little nervy and shy, but dressed in swirls of pink and blue the pair looked totally unstoppable. And no one was more diva-fierce than Valentina, with her unicorn Cinder, riding in on a studded leather saddle.

Now the Fate Fairies were ready for their very last transformation: "Sophia and Wildstar!"

Sophia stepped underneath the arch and instantly felt a burst of magical energy rush through her body. Her friends from Sapphire dorm started cheering.

Sophia's ripped jeans and beanie were gone. Instead she was wearing a stunning gold and purple riding outfit that was embellished with stars. Wildstar whickered joyfully, rearing up to reveal an amazing gold saddle with swirls of rainbow colour.

"These 'uniforms' are certainly a change from tradition," remarked Ms Furi.

Ms Primrose tried to hide her smile. "It seems that the Fate Fairies feel this class has a lot of *personality*."

Ms Furi huffed grumpily as the students led their unicorns out to the stables. The bright airy buildings came alive with noisy whoops, chatter and laughter as everyone *oohed* and *aahed* over the amazing spaces. Just like the dormitories, every stable had been expertly customised to suit the unicorn that would live there.

"It's so beautiful," gasped Sophia, as they walked into Sapphire dorm's stable. "And a little different to the barn at home!"

Wildstar snickered good-naturedly as if to tell her, "This will do just fine".

The stable was circular, with rafters draped in gorgeous summer flowers. There were plentiful baskets of Sky Berries for the unicorns to eat and a well of cool, turquoise water in the centre. Fernakus the Dwerpin was waiting to meet them, floating through the air on an adorable flying pig called Petula.

"Jiminy Flipmouse," he exclaimed, "those are some top-notch unicorns! The magical water flowing here from Starglow Lake will keep them in tip-top shape. Trust me, they're in good hands!"

Sophia nodded gratefully, then guided Wildstar into her stall.

"What do you think?" she asked.

Wildstar took in the round windows, the soft straw bedding and the twinkling stars hanging down from the ceiling.

"Those stars! They're like my pendant," said Sophia, taking it out to show the unicorn. "Dad used to call me his shining star, but maybe you already knew that?"

Wildstar's eyes grew tender. She placed her muzzle in Sophia's hands and the pair stayed like that for a moment, silently remembering.

"OK," decided Sophia at last. "You better get some rest – training starts tomorrow. We're going to bond, you'll get your magic back and I'm going to be a great Unicorn Rider, just like my dad. Sound like a plan?"

CHAPTER EIGHT

Trouble was brewing in the gloomy depths of the Crystal Caves. Ravenzella, the banished Queen of Grimoria, was tired of being locked away, out of sight. She thought about the unicorns and their riders every day and every night, rage growing inside her. Crimsette the Shadow Sprite and Ash the ogre watched their mistress pace up and down inside the quartz bars of the Cell of Eternity, purple eyes flashing, as she plotted and planned.

"I didn't expect eternal imprisonment to be pleasant," she grumbled. "But not being able to use my magic is so painfully boring."

Ash tried to be helpful. "Wanna play a game? I spy, with my ogre eye…"

"Be gone!" screeched Ravenzella, sending him scuttling into the shadows.

The queen raised her hands to cast a blast of Grim Magic in Ash's direction but, as always, the spell dissolved into nothing the instant it touched the crystal cell wall.

"Gah!" she screeched, for the thousandth time.

Crimsette flitted out of the darkness and hovered as close to the cage as she dared.

"I cannot wait to get you out of this place," she whined in her queen's ear. "The unicorns must not be allowed to humiliate you any longer!"

Ravenzella stamped her foot. Her time had come. Although *she* remained trapped in a rotten underground prison, there were others who could fight back. Ash and Crimsette lined up in front of the cell and waited for their instructions.

"You both know what I need," she said, icily. "Get it. After that I will finally be able to finish what I started and take my revenge on Unicorn Academy."

The trio howled with laughter. Ash and Crimsette stole away into the night, leaving the Queen of Grimoria smirking at her cleverness.

The next morning, Sophia and her friends put on their uniforms and made their way down to the stables.

"Hi Wildstar!" said Sophia cheerfully, holding her hand out to reveal some fresh Sky Berries for the unicorn to nibble.

Wildstar wandered out of her stall, whickering hello before snuffling up the berries. Fernakus had explained that Sky Berries grew on the mountain slopes of the island. The fruit was the best food for unicorns, containing all the vitamins and minerals they needed to stay healthy and strong.

As soon they were ready, Sophia and Wildstar followed the others out to the training field. Everybody was excited to be finally having a riding lesson. There were lots of different abilities in the class, but each student had been picked for a reason – a special quality that meant they had the potential to become a Unicorn Rider. As they waited for the teacher, Ms Wildwood, to begin, Sophia couldn't help overhearing the other students whispering behind their hands and sneaking glances at her. The news about her talk with Ms Primrose must have spread. She caught Ava's eye and beckoned her over.

"I guess the whole 'daughter-of-the-guy-who-took-down-Ravenzella' thing is out of the bag then?" she smiled.

"It is a pretty awesome story," nodded Ava. "It's like you're riding in his footsteps!"

Valentina scoffed dismissively as she held onto Cinder's bridle.

"You dad might be some hero, or whatever," she said, rolling her eyes. "But you? I don't see it."

Wildstar whinnied and stamped her hoof. Sophia frowned, but then noticed Ava, Layla, Isabel and Rory grouping themselves around her, and suddenly she felt strong.

"Uh-oh," said Isabel, winking at her friend. "It sounds like someone's jealous."

"Jealous?" snapped Valentina. "The Furi family legacy goes back generations. This is *my* academy. Got it?"

"Oh, is it?" piped up Rory. "Does that mean it's you I need to talk to about the quality of the toilet paper?"

Valentina blushed fiercely, then stalked across

to the opposite side of the training field. Sophia and Rory shared a silly grin.

The chatter soon died down when Ms Wildwood mounted her unicorn, Rush, and rode into the centre of the field.

"Are you all ready to have some fun?" she called.

Sophia felt her cheeks flush with excitement. She couldn't wait to get back in a saddle again! Poor Layla didn't look quite so sure.

Ms Wildwood continued. "Congratulations on finding your matches. To stay at this academy you'll have to bond with your unicorn, and the first step is learning how to ride. Some of you might be a little nervous. It's important to..."

Layla's hand shot up as her words tumbled out. "...stay calm. Unicorns can feel your energy."

"That's right, Layla," nodded Ms Wildwood. "When you're ready to climb on, just..."

Layla's hand was up again. "...hold the reins, push up and ease down slowly into the saddle."

Sophia smiled at Isabel. "She stayed up all night reading the Sparklebook, didn't she?"

"Oh yes," Isabel replied.

With so much knowledge in the class, Ms Wildwood decided it might be better for the students to press on and get started. The students lined up in a row, ready to mount their unicorns. A nervous hush fell across the field. Unicorns were wild animals. Even the more confident riders felt cautious next to these powerful, unpredictable creatures.

"Stay calm, stay calm," muttered Ava, her legs trembling as she stepped alongside Leaf. Without a word of instruction, the unicorn quietly dipped her head, allowing her rider to get on with ease. Ava squealed with delight.

Sophia smiled at Leaf's kindness, but when she

approached Wildstar, the unicorn folded right down to her knees, giving her an even easier way to get on.

"Thanks," said Sophia, as Wildstar gently rose back up to her full height, "but it's OK. I've ridden lots of times – I can mount by myself."

Wildstar flicked her ears and walked forward as if she hadn't heard.

Once everyone was safely in their saddles, Ms Wildwood asked the class to trot around the training field. Valentina immediately took the lead, guiding Cinder with ease. It was clear she had been riding for years. Ava was not so steady, and while Isabel was ready to race, her unicorn, River, seemed more interested in dawdling in the grass and munching on dandelions.

Sophia took a deep breath, then pressed her legs against Wildstar's body. The unicorn instantly moved forward, progressing from a lively trot into a graceful, rolling gallop.

"Well done, Wildstar," whispered Sophia. "Well done!"

Ms Wildwood nodded and smiled. Sophia was clearly a natural, but despite doing hours of homework, poor Layla was not. While Glacier moved effortlessly around the training field at a jaunty pace, her rider was barely clinging on.

"Help!" shouted Layla, trying not to fall.

"Rush, we've got a runner," announced Ms Wildwood, spurring her unicorn to the rescue.

A burst of sparkly magic fizzed around Rush's hooves, and he was off, rounding Glacier up with ease and bringing her back to a halt.

"Thanks!" said Layla, breathlessly. "That didn't go according to the Sparklebook."

After everyone had got a bit more practice, the more confident riders were allowed to have a go at the jumping rings. Valentina and Cinder soared through the highest ring time after time, showing off their amazing skills.

"We can do that too, Wildstar," said Sophia. "Let's ride!"

She turned her reins towards the highest jumping ring and focused her eyes. But when she urged Wildstar forward, the unicorn deliberately swerved and skipped slowly through the very lowest ring instead.

"Awww," mocked Valentina, "she's starting you on the kiddie ring."

Sophia waited until Valentina had ridden off, so she could take a minute alone with Wildstar.

"I know my dad was an amazing rider and you think I am a newbie," she said, dismounting so they could look into each other's eyes. "But trust me – I have skills."

Wildstar huffed and turned her head away.

Cr-ack!

Sophia was about to try again, when she heard something moving in the trees at the edge of the field. Wildstar's ears slid back as she sniffed the air – she had heard it, too! There was something out there, watching them.

"Come on," said Sophia. "Let's check it out."

But when she stepped out towards the forest, Wildstar swiftly moved in front of her, blocking her path. Whichever way Sophia went, Wildstar was there, standing in her way.

"You do know I am training to be a Unicorn Rider, right?" frowned Sophia, frustrated. "Protectors of the island? Saving magic for the entire world? You have got to trust me!"

Wildstar would not budge. Giving up, Sophia wearily climbed onto her unicorn and trotted back towards the class.

Ash and Crimsette waited until Ms Wildwood's

lesson had finished, then peeked out from between the trees.

"We missed our chance this time," grumbled Crimsette. "But we'll be back..."

After lunch, it was time for Ms Rosemary's unicorn care and grooming lesson. Ms Rosemary was the youngest teacher in the academy, and rode a slender palomino unicorn called Rhapsody. While Fernakus handed out grooming tools, Rhapsody used her Music Magic to fill the stable with lovely, relaxing melodies.

Sophia watched, spellbound, as the Dwerpin dropped a star-covered brush and a small purple bottle into her out-stretched hands.

"A Carebrush for a little care and flair," he explained merrily. "And Winklewash for a sparkletastic clean!"

"Thanks, Fernakus!" Sophia filled a bucket with

water, grabbed a sponge and got to work. "I am going to make you cleaner than you've ever been in your whole life!" she promised Wildstar, squeezing three giant blobs of shampoo into the bucket.

Quick as a flash, Wildstar grabbed the bottle in her teeth and lifted it out of Sophia's reach.

"Hey you!" shouted Sophia. "I know what I'm doing! I washed Mary Lou all the ti—"

Pink, pearly bubbles of Winklewash began to pop and swell in the bucket. In seconds the magical soap suds had puffed up and up, filling the whole stable with a big, bubbly mess.

"Sophia!" called Ms Rosemary. "You're only supposed to use *one* drop of Winklewash!"

Sophia hoped that the bubbles would at least hide her blushes. Wildstar snorted crossly. Maybe she still had a few things to learn about unicorns.

In the stall next door, Ava was having a much better time. Leaf had been washed, scrubbed and brushed until her coat gleamed. The unicorn closed her eyes blissfully as Ava ran the Carebrush through her beautiful violet and turquoise mane, until suddenly they both began to shimmer with a soft glowing light. Rhapsody's music faded, replaced by the whooshing sound of sparkles encircling both unicorn and rider.

"Ava!"

The glittering magic was so powerful it took Sophia's breath away. At last it cleared, and Ava cried out in surprise. Luminous streaks of violet had appeared in her hair, the exact same shade as the locks running through Leaf's mane and tail. Leaf joyfully raised her spiralling horn up into the air as magical plant-like swirls and butterflies appeared across her body. Thick, flowery vines burst out of the ground before her, lifting a very

99

surprised Fernakus up into the air.

"Plant Magic!" he laughed, trying to keep his balance. "An enchanting power indeed!"

Sophia gradually began to understand what was happening. Leaf had found her magic, and bonded with Ava. This was the highest form of friendship, the most important step in becoming a Unicorn Rider. She ran over to Ava and stopped beside her.

"Congratulations," she said. "You did it."

"Thanks!" Ava replied. "I just know you and Wildstar will be the next ones to bond."

As kind as always, Ava truly meant every word. Sophia, however, was not feeling quite so sure.

$$\ast \, \ast \, \ast$$

CHAPTER NINE

The first week of training was challenging. All Sophia wanted to do was ride – to show the world what she could do. Wildstar, it seemed, had other ideas. Her unicorn match was friendly enough, but Sophia could tell that she didn't trust her yet. It felt as if everyone else in Sapphire dorm seemed to be getting closer to their unicorns, leaving Sophia to watch from the back as they galloped further and further ahead. This really wasn't how things were meant to be. Didn't Wildstar know how much she had to offer, that she was ready to shine?

"I get the feeling you don't think I can do this," Sophia sighed one afternoon as she and Wildstar watched Rory and Storm tearing around the academy race track, flurries of dust kicking up behind them.

Wildstar snorted breezily.

"I'm the daughter of the best Unicorn Rider ever!" Sophia insisted. "*He* was the one who taught me how to ride. You do know that, don't you? And if we don't bond soon, I'll be sent..."

Sophia was interrupted by a terrified squeal from the other side of the field. It had come from a unicorn – River. Sophia saw Isabel struggling to stay in her seat as the spooked unicorn pranced from hoof to hoof. Ms Rosemary cantered over at once, but even Rhapsody looked frightened.

"What are *those*?"

Two furry creatures shaped like enormous balls of fluff were hopping across the field, devouring everything in their path. Their adorable appearance did not seem to match their destructive behaviour at all. In fact, Sophia had never seen anything move so fast. Hay bales, buckets of Sky Berries, even fence posts were being gobbled up in moments. She felt Wildstar's body stiffen with nerves.

"Everybody stay calm," instructed Ms Rosemary, desperately trying to stop Rhapsody from bolting. "Those are Fluffhoppers. They're not easy to catch."

Even from across the field, Sophia could tell this was an emergency. The Fluffhoppers split off in different directions, wreaking havoc with every bound. Sophia spotted Isabel speaking urgently in River's ear. River's eyes were wide, unsure, but on his rider's command he sprang into a gallop.

"That's it!" shouted Isabel, leaning forward as they rode into the wind. "You've so got this!"

And somehow, River began to believe it. The beautiful blue stallion raced with such intensity, he let out a whinny of pure joy, thrilled to discover what he could do. A magical shimmer of popping stars and light started to swirl around them as they galloped. Sophia spotted strands of electric blue appear in Isabel's blonde ponytail and realised they were bonding.

"Yes!" cheered Isabel. "My unicorn is awesome!"

Proudly and with confidence, River lifted his pink unicorn horn up towards the sky. His new magical markings glowed brightly as swirls of magic danced up and down his majestic horn. A sparkling flash of magic pulled a fountain of water from the stream at the side of the training ground. The water gushed over one of the runaway Fluffhoppers, encasing it in a big, transparent bubble.

Sophia gasped. River's power was Water

Magic! She wanted to ride over and say well done, but there wasn't time for that – the second Fluffhopper was now chomping and leaping its way towards the academy building. Valentina and Cinder took off after it.

"This is our chance, Wildstar," Sophia whispered, shaking her reins. "Let's catch it!"

Reluctantly, Wildstar cantered forward, trailing after Valentina and Cinder. Sophia urged her faster and faster, until at last they were neck and neck. The Fluffhopper zigged and zagged through the academy gardens, before bouncing over the bubbling moat that wound around the central courtyard and academy entrance.

A little way behind, Sophia and Valentina glared at one another, each determined to be the one to succeed. With an extra surge of effort, Sophia managed to take the lead. She turned her focus on the water up ahead, leaned deeper into

Wildstar's saddle and got ready to jump.

"Whoa!"

Sophia was sent tumbling forward over Wildstar's neck, landing on the ground with a bump. The unicorn had refused to jump for her! Wildstar quickly nuzzled her rider to check that she wasn't hurt, then stood stubbornly rooted to the spot. All Sophia could do was watch as Valentina and Cinder vaulted over their heads, rounding up the Fluffhopper in an amazing display of skill and speed.

While Ms Furi rode up to help take the furry pest away, sparks of red light whizzed and flashed around Valentina and her unicorn. Sophia's heart fell. Of all the students to bond next, did it have to be Valentina? Cinder shot a swirl of Fire Magic from his horn as his rider's hair began to glow with flame-coloured streaks.

"Well done!" exclaimed Ms Furi. "Ms Rosemary

informed me that we had a Fluffhopper situation, but I can see that Isabel and Valentina have impressively controlled it ... and bonded."

Valentina preened in triumph.

"You'll both get extra credit for this in my magical creatures class," Ms Furi went on.

"Thank you, Auntie!" said Valentina, before hastily adding, "I mean, *Ms Furi.*"

Sophia bit her lip. Her own dreams had never felt so far away.

"Better get packed," sniped Valentina, as she rode past her. "The last fairy boat off the island leaves at six."

The class headed back to the stables, while Sophia struggled to get back on her feet. Wildstar tried to help her up with her nose, but Sophia shrugged her away.

"I thought we were in this together?" she said, glumly. "What happened to the plan? Don't you *want* your magic back?"

Wildstar's eyes widened. For a moment, Sophia could almost see all the feelings swirling around inside her unicorn.

"When we matched I thought you were a second chance to have a piece of my dad with me," she whispered, struggling to keep back her tears. "But maybe the Fate Fairy made a mistake. You obviously don't think I am worth bonding with."

Sophia passed Wildstar's reins back to her, and then slowly walked away.

That evening, Ava and Sophia had a long talk on the balcony. Ava couldn't bear to see her friend looking so heartbroken. After their lessons, Sophia had checked Wildstar was safe in her stable, then gone straight up to their room. Even Rory's jokes couldn't cheer her up. Wildstar was such a beautiful unicorn, Ava wished she could find a way for her friend to get close to her.

"How can I bond if Wildstar won't let me show her how good a rider I am?" Sophia spluttered.

"I think bonding with a unicorn might be about more than just riding," Ava said kindly. "It's about connecting, understanding each other. It's like getting to know a friend."

Sophia's eyes filled with sadness. "The friend thing isn't really my speciality. I haven't had a lot of them since…"

Ava looked puzzled. "Since what?"

"When my dad died, I didn't want to feel that kind of hurt ever again," Sophia admitted. "Getting close to someone and losing them was the worst. So I decided that I'd be better off just being me. On my own."

Sophia clasped her star pendant tightly, then hung her head.

"Maybe," Ava said quietly, edging a little closer to her friend, "you and Wildstar have something in common. She was probably hurt when she lost your dad, too. Maybe she's being extra protective of you because she feels like she couldn't protect your dad?"

Sophia's head shot up. She hadn't thought of it that way. "Oh! So it's not that Wildstar doesn't trust me. It's that she doesn't trust herself."

Suddenly everything fell into place. Poor Wildstar! Sophia had to talk to her, to say sorry, to tell her she understood.

Neeeeigh!

A haunting, high-pitched squeal echoed across the academy grounds.

"Wildstar?"

Sophia and Ava exchanged worried glances. The sound of fear had come from the stables. The girls raced along the landing – they had to get down there!

"Did you hear that?" squeaked Layla, poking her head out of her bedroom. "What's happening?"

Sophia, Ava and Layla took less than a minute to rush down to the Sapphire stable building, hearts pounding in their chests. Outside, Ava noticed a barrel, shaking and rocking as if someone was banging from the inside. She prised open the lid and discovered poor Fernakus trapped at the bottom.

"Fernakus!" said Sophia, urgently. "What happened?"

The Dwerpin smiled weakly as the girls helped pull him out. "I was cleaning Carebrushes one minute and tossed in a barrel like a rotten Sky Berry the next!"

Inside the stables, more unicorns began to bray and call. Something felt terribly wrong.

Sophia charged inside.

"Wildstar!" she shouted. "Where's Wildstar?"

The other unicorns tossed their manes and stomped their hooves, eyes wide with fear. Wildstar was nowhere to be seen.

"I am sorry," said Fernakus, hurrying in behind her. "It was a Shadow Sprite and an ogre. They took her away!"

"Oh no!" gasped Layla, remembering what she'd read in the Sparklebook. "They're part of Ravenzella's army!"

"Did they *say* anything?" pleaded Sophia. "Where are they taking her?"

Fernakus's voice was still shaky. "It was all so fast, b-b-ut I believe they mentioned the Crystal Caves."

"But the caves are off-limits to academy students," interjected Layla.

"I don't care," said Sophia. "I've got to

save Wildstar!"

Ava was already running to fetch Leaf's saddle. "I'm coming with you!"

Layla looked across at Glacier. The unicorn pawed the ground impatiently with her hoof. "I guess now would be a good time to start breaking the rules," she admitted. "You can ride with me, Sophia."

Sophia crouched down and took Fernakus's hands. "Please. Tell Ms Primrose."

"Of course!" The Dwerpin nodded and hurried away.

As soon as Ava and Leaf were ready, Sophia climbed up onto Glacier's back, and put her arms around Layla's tummy.

The unicorns turned away from the academy and its glimmering white marble towers. It was time to ride into the darkness of the night.

★ ★ ★

CHAPTER TEN

Sophia had never galloped this fast before. Leaf and Glacier thundered along the trail with the wind streaming through their manes and only the flickering light of the stars to guide them. The unicorns charged past crescent beaches, over rolling hills and on towards the snowy mountains on the far side of the island. As she clung on to Layla's waist, all Sophia could think about was Wildstar. Her unicorn would be feeling so frightened and alone right now. Sophia wished that she could have the chance to tell her how sorry she was, to explain that she understood.

"Whoa!"

Ava brought Leaf up to a sharp halt. The unicorns had reached a rocky incline at the edge of a deep ravine. Ahead of them was a bridge encrusted with scarlet gemstones. It glinted mysteriously, swaying gently from side to side. Sophia dared herself to peep down over Glacier's shoulder, then shuddered and pulled back. The ravine was so deep she couldn't see the bottom – only blackness.

"According to the Sparklebook, this is Phoenix Bridge," said Layla. "The Crystal Caves are just on the other side."

Leaf gingerly put one hoof onto the bridge, carefully leading the group across.

"Fluffy bunnies, glitter pens, baby goats wearing pyjamas..." muttered Ava, keeping her eyes shut tight.

"Are you OK?" called Sophia, as Glacier

followed behind.

"Just a little scared of heights," replied Ava. "I'm trying to think happy thoughts to keep calm."

Whoosh!

A bat flew up from the chasm below, flapping right into their faces. Glacier neighed in shock and reared up on her hind legs, landing back down on the bridge with such force that one of the posts securing the walkway was dragged out of the ground.

"Help!"

The riders and their unicorns slipped back along the bridge and off the edge. Ava, Layla and Sophia screamed as they fell, tumbling towards the black hole beneath them. Everything happened so quickly, Sophia couldn't tell what was up and what was down. Just when she was certain they were all doomed, Leaf summoned a petal-fizzing swirl of Plant Magic. Curling green vines shot out from the ravine walls surrounding them, wrapping around the bridge at one end, and curling around the riders and the unicorns at the other.

"Nice catch, Leaf!" gasped Sophia, as they dangled above the blackness.

Ava pointed at the remaining post that was holding the bridge up. It had begun to come loose and was now sliding towards the edge, too.

"What do we do now?"

"Well, it's totally not cool that you snuck out of school to have fun without me," announced a familiar voice. "I was just about to pull an epic sequel to my unicorn undies prank, when I saw you ride off."

Sophia, Ava and Layla all shouted at once: "RORY!"

The post slid a little closer to the edge. Rory eyed the other side of the bridge, then leaned over the saddle to speak to Storm.

"Alright girl. We're both excellent at having fun," he whispered, "but now we've got to try the hero thing and get to that post. Are you up for it?"

Storm whinnied fearlessly, then backed away from the edge of the ravine so she could get a running start.

"It's too far!" warned Layla, realising what she was about to attempt. "You won't make it!"

But Storm had already pushed herself off. Rory and his unicorn sailed over the chasm, landing hard against the rock on the other side. Rory clung to Storm's back as she struggled to hang onto the edge.

"You can do this," he urged. "I know you can."

Rory's confidence in Storm gave her the extra burst of energy she needed. The unicorn pushed both hooves up the rock and hauled herself over the edge using all the strength she had. As she dragged them to safety, sparks of indigo light swooshed around Rory and Storm, binding them together in a magical blur. The unicorn crashed her foot against the ground and a lightning bolt flashed overhead – her Weather Magic had arrived, along with bold lightning bolt markings across her body.

"This is even cooler than I thought!" gasped Rory, as streaks of icy blue began to appear in his hair. "Storm! We've bonded!"

Storm crashed her foot down one more time, pounding the post back into the ground in one thunderous stomp.

"I think we need a new bridge," directed Rory, "Hit that tree, Storm!"

The unicorn sent a lightning blast towards a withered tree growing up beside the ravine, dropping the trunk across the gorge to form a natural gangplank. Leaf and Glacier scrambled along it, with Ava, Layla and Sophia clinging to their backs.

"That was amazing!" gasped Sophia, when they had all reached solid ground. "Thank you."

Layla pointed to a ghostly pine forest rising out of the valley below.

"The Crystal Caves are that way," she said.

"Let's keep going," nodded Sophia.

The forest was unlike anything they had ever seen before. Jagged trees towered above them, formed out of sparkling, frost-white diamonds. Each one was as tall as a church spire, covered with spiky branches that prickled and scratched. After several minutes of hard riding, the unicorns got to the other side.

"I think we're here," said Ava, pointing to a misty moat encircling the entrance to the Crystal Caves.

The only way to cross the moat was to leap across chunks of breaking crystal, avoiding the threatening mass of Crystal Crocodiles that emerged from the waters below. Leaf, Glacier and Storm nervously picked their way across, narrowly missing the crocs' sharp, snapping teeth. When they got to the entrance of the Crystal Caves, the riders dismounted and led the way inside.

It felt very, very cold. Icy water trickled down the walls and deep gem-coloured crystals cast an eerie sheen. Sophia made a shushing sound, and then signalled for everyone to duck out of sight. She had spotted the flickering glow of the Cell of Eternity just up ahead.

"Wildstar!"

Sophia was devastated to see that her unicorn was there, chained up beside Ravenzella's prison. She could feel her heart panic, desperate to find a way to get her friend away from their sworn enemy.

"What a delightfully dreamy day!"

A caped figure popped up behind them and took off his hood. Sophia felt a rush of relief to see Fernakus.

"Thank goodness you're here!" she whispered. "Where's Ms Primrose?"

"I decided not to tell her," said the Dwerpin, greeting Sophia with a hard smile. "Ravenzella! Our visitors have arrived."

"Fernakus!" hissed Rory. "What are you doing?"

Sophia was flabbergasted. "Are you *helping* Ravenzella? I thought you were our friend?"

"I do feel terrible about it," Fernakus replied, not very sincerely. "But when the opportunity presented itself, I thought maybe I'm a Dwerpin who's meant for more than cleaning Carebrushes and picking Sky Berries."

"That stuff matters!" burst out Ava.

The commotion caught Crimsette's attention. The Shadow Sprite cackled spitefully when she spotted the new arrivals.

"Thanks for the delivery, *Fernyguts*!" she screeched. "They're all yours, Ash."

SMASH!

The ogre hurled a massive chunk of crystal at the wall behind the unicorns and it collapsed instantly, creating an avalanche of sparkling stone. Wildstar whinnied in fright to see that Sophia was buried on one side of the huge pile of debris, with her friends trapped on the other.

"Sophia! Sophia!" screamed Ava, turning to Layla and Rory. "Help me dig! She's on her own over there with Ravenzella!"

Ava, Layla and Rory flung the rubble aside with their hands, trying to make a gap in the wall. The unicorns helped as best they could, loosening more and more rocks until ... *CRASH!* ... the ground caved in, sending them falling down to a grotto below, at the edge of a fast-moving underground river.

Layla and Glacier landed on the shore, but Ava, Rory, Leaf and Storm were not so lucky. The chunk of rock they were standing on broke away and began to float down the river.

"Help, Layla!" shouted Rory. "Quickly!"

Layla pulled the Sparklebook out of Glacier's saddlebag.

"There has to be something in here that can help," she muttered, frantically flipping through the pages. "I don't know what to do!"

Glacier bumped the Sparklebook with her nose, flipping it shut. Her eyes narrowed with determination and courage, and at last Layla got the message.

"OK, I get it," she admitted, climbing back

onto Glacier's saddle. "There's no time for the Sparklebook. Let's ride!"

Layla was not the best rider, but her courage was unstoppable. Glacier galloped along the river edge, with Layla ducking and swerving to avoid the sharp crystals jutting out of the walls. Riding as one, the pair went faster and faster until a shimmer of brilliant lilac magic lit up the cave around them. Snowflakes sparkled all over Glacier's coat, and Layla's curls tumbled with locks of purple and blue.

"We're bonding!" cried Layla. "And it's way better in real life than in the books!"

The pair sped up even more, until they were finally level with their friends. Layla saw that the river plunged down into a waterfall not far ahead, but she tried not to be afraid. Instead, she buried her head in Glacier's mane and whispered, "Do you have magic now?"

Glacier raised her head, sending a jet of Ice Magic across the water. The river instantly froze, meaning Rory, Ava, and their unicorns, could scramble to safety.

"We have to get out of here," said Layla, giving them each a high-five. "We must help Sophia and Wildstar before Ravenzella does something terrible."

✦ ✦ ✦

CHAPTER ELEVEN

Sophia crouched behind a pile of fallen crystals, nervously holding her breath. Just metres away from her, Ash was tossing aside huge shards of rock as if they were tiny twigs.

"Where are you?" grunted the ogre, stomping closer. "The queen is waiting!"

Sophia was able to stay out of sight for a little while, until a tiny shadow flickered above her head. Crimsette darted down to her eye level and smirked: "You stink at hide and seek."

Ash lumbered over to the Shadow Sprite, reached down with his massive arm and pulled

Sophia out by the foot. He carried her, struggling and twisting, to the Cell of Eternity, and dropped her onto the ground. Wildstar fought to help Sophia, pulling furiously against her chains.

"Here's the girl, your Magnificence!" piped up Fernakus.

Ravenzella ignored the Dwerpin, preferring to watch with amusement as Sophia tried to soothe the frantic unicorn.

"How sweet!" she cackled. "In an icky sort of way."

"If you hurt her," threatened Sophia. "I'll—"

"Tell a teacher on me?" suggested Ravenzella, her face creasing up with pleasure. "Or use your unicorn magic perhaps? Oh, that's right ... you two haven't bonded yet. I'm simply *terrified*."

Ash and Crimsette snickered. The Queen of Grimoria leered at Sophia, smiling a cold, bitter smile.

"You have your father's eyes."

Sophia refused to turn her head away, glaring at Ravenzella as she continued to speak.

"I remember him very well, you see. He was the Unicorn Rider who locked me away in this infernal cell."

Fernakus stuck up his hand. "You'll be out in the blink of a wink, oh pointy one! I'll deliver the key as promised."

"The key?" Sophia stepped away from the cage walls, trying to guard her unicorn. "Wildstar will *never* show you where the key is!"

Ravenzella shrieked with laughter. "It's already here," she replied sweetly. "Taking your pet was just my clever way of getting you to bring the key to me." She nodded sharply at Crimsette, who quick as a flash buzzed over and snatched the star pendant from Sophia's neck.

"No!" she yelled, but the necklace was already

dangling from the queen's spiky fingers.

"My hairy little helper told me that the key had returned to the island as soon as you arrived," said Ravenzella, gesturing at Fernakus.

"The key can't be my pendant," insisted Sophia. "That's *mine*!"

"I know it is," Ravenzella shot back. "From your father, yes?"

Sophia lunged at the queen, but it was hopeless. Ash used all his ogre strength to hold her back, allowing Ravenzella to insert the star-shaped pendant into a slot at the centre of a glistening cluster of crystals. The formation shone with light and the Cell of Eternity disappeared.

Ravenzella stepped victoriously from her prison. As she pulled herself up to her full height, Sophia noticed the purple swirls of Grim Magic curling ominously around her. Ravenzella eyed Wildstar with disdain.

"The most powerful, magical creatures?" she sneered. "Ha! Their devotion to goodness is pathetic. It's time for all Unicorn Riders to pay the price for making my home of Grimoria disappear. It's time to make their precious unicorns vanish! But first, Sophia, let's make sure that *you* have no chance of interfering."

With a wave of her hands, the queen conjured a dark spell. She threw her arms forward, preparing to blast it at Sophia, but Wildstar burst out of her chains and leapt in front of her rider.

The blast hit the unicorn with such power, the walls around them began to shatter and crack. Wildstar slumped to the ground, wounded. Sophia watched, aghast, as her unicorn began to fade away.

"No!" she sobbed. "Please!"

"Take your daddy's precious gift!" barked

Ravenzella, hurling the necklace back at her. "I'd like to say it's nothing personal ... but it is."

And with that, the Queen of Grimoria used her dark powers to vanish from the collapsing cavern, taking Ash and Crimsette with her. Fernakus was left to fend for himself. The sly Dwerpin scuttled out of the tunnel without giving Sophia a backwards glance.

Wildstar lay on her side, slipping away with every passing moment.

"What's happening to you?" sobbed Sophia, using her body to try to protect the unicorn from the avalanche of crystals falling all around them. When the jagged rocks finally stopped tumbling, the pair were cramped into a tiny pocket of space. Wildstar was growing weak, but somehow she managed to turn her head towards a narrow opening in the corner. She whinnied encouragingly. The gap was just about big enough for Sophia to crawl through.

Sophia shook her head. "I'm not leaving without you!"

There was another loud crack, and the ceiling sunk a little lower. It wouldn't hold out for long. Sophia took a deep breath and tried to put into words everything that she was holding inside her heart.

"I'm sorry," she whispered, stroking the unicorn's forehead. "All you've been doing is trying to protect me. I know how much you miss my dad. I do, too. But you never really lost him. He lives in you, Wildstar."

The unicorn looked up at Sophia through fading eyes. The words meant everything to her.

"And you don't have to be afraid of losing me, either," Sophia added, "'cause I'm with you 'til the end." Sophia laid her head on Wildstar's chest, crying softly. "Please don't go. You *are* my destiny."

More rocks crashed and abruptly the chamber caved in. Everything was pitch-black, until, suddenly, a streak of bright, dazzling light burst out through the cracks...

* * *

CHAPTER TWELVE

Ava, Rory, Layla and their unicorns felt the caves quiver and shake. Gem-hard shards of crystal tumbled around them, forming huge mounds of glittering rubble.

"I'm worried about Sophia and Wildstar," said Ava. "How are we are going to get to them now?"

Before anyone could answer, a fantastic explosion of rainbow light blasted the cave wall wide open. A kaleidoscope of reds, yellows, blues and violets filled the chamber, and crystals everywhere glittered and shone. The friends were astonished to see Wildstar galloping across a rainbow with Sophia on her back. The unicorn looked more vivid and majestic than ever as she reached the end of the colourful arch, her Light Magic flowing through her.

"They're safe!" gasped Ava.

"And they've *bonded*," added Layla, noticing the glowing streaks of rainbow colours running through Sophia's hair and the pattern of stars that sparkled across Wildstar's shimmering body.

Sophia beamed with happiness. "The Fate Fairy was right. We make a perfect match!"

Wildstar reared on her back legs and whinnied, glowing even more brightly than before.

"You have Light Magic!" said Rory. "That's so cool!"

Now that they were together again, the four friends needed to focus on getting out of the caves. Layla led the way, and when they got to the cave entrance Glacier used her

Ice Magic to freeze the moat so they could scramble out into the night air.

"That is awesome!" cried Sophia. "Tonight we're going to need all the magic we can get. Ravenzella is free and she wants to get rid of every unicorn on this island."

"She won't if we have anything to do with it," promised Ava.

Rory urged Storm to gallop even faster. "Let's go!"

But Ravenzella had already arrived at the Unicorn Academy and was putting her powers to bad use.

"Those Unicorn Riders should never have messed with me," she told Ash and Crimsette.

Purple, smoky tendrils of Grim Magic were snaking all over the academy grounds and stables, covering everything in a shadowy web.

Any unicorn the spell touched began to weaken and fade away.

Valentina and Isabel were returning from a ride on Cinder and River when they noticed the strange, gloomy cloud draped over the stables.

"Quick!" hissed Valentina. "Let's hide."

The girls and their unicorns disappeared into the gardens, taking care to stay close enough to overhear Ravenzella's screeches.

"Let's go to Starglow Lake," she cackled. "I'm going to wipe out the rest of the unicorns on this repulsive island."

Ravenzella and her lackies rose into the air on a wave of Grim Magic, eager to inflict even more damage.

Whoosh!

Suddenly, a burst of rainbow light blasted the villains back down to the ground.

"I like this place the way it is," a voice said, firmly.

Isabel and Valentina peeped out of their hiding place, clapped their hands over their mouths in shock, then ducked back out of view.

"Did you see?" Isabel whispered to Valentina. "It's Sophia!"

"She's ... *changed*," Valentina said softly, taking in Wildstar's brave eyes and dazzling magical markings.

Just then Ava, Layla and Rory appeared behind Sophia. The four Unicorn Riders were united, gazing purposefully at the Queen of Grimoria.

"I see you have your father's persistence," Ravenzella sneered at Sophia. "He was annoying, too."

Ravenzella opened her hands to the sky. Isabel and Valentina watched secretly as waves of Grim Magic poured down from her palms like waterfalls of inky water. The queen was lifted up and up, while blasts of purple darkness rained down on Sophia and her friends.

"Go Wildstar!" shouted Sophia, expertly moving the reins to help her unicorn dodge the shadows. Wildstar's gold horn shone brightly. Her Light Magic could deflect the worst of the blasts, but Ravenzella was relentless. She laughed mercilessly, then cast out a new shadow that shaped itself into a ball of darkness. The ball grew a head, arms and legs – transforming into a towering shadow creature made out of Grim Magic.

"How do you like that?" Ravenzella dared the girl, her eyes blazing with malice.

"We can handle one giant shadow creature," shot back Sophia.

The shadow creature began to lumber towards Sophia and Wildstar, but then split itself into five more identical monsters. Ravenzella's dark army marched on, ripping trees out of the ground and hurling them into the air.

"Uh-oh," muttered Sophia.

Wildstar danced back a few steps.

Sophia was desperately trying to work out what to do next when a red-hot fireball whistled past them, hitting one of the shadow creatures full in the chest. It puffed away into nothingness. *"Who did that?"* she wondered.

"Apparently you need some help," said Valentina coolly, riding up on Cinder.

"I wish I could say I don't," grinned Sophia, "but thanks."

Isabel rode forward too, her face full of purpose.

"We can handle these shadow creeps!" she declared, leaning down to rub her unicorn's neck. "Can't we, River?"

141

With Isabel and Valentina on their side, the battle was more even. The academy riders and their brave unicorns summoned all of their magic powers, determined to stop Ravenzella from ruining their world. River used his Water Magic to wash the shadow creatures away, while Glacier used Ice Magic to make the ground so slippery it sent Ash crashing onto his back. Storm swiftly bowed her head and an unstoppable gust of wind came swirling out of her horn, sending the ogre spinning into a massive mound of snow. Leaf used her Plant Magic to send vines spinning like lassoes, knocking out more shadow creatures and sending Crimsette fluttering for cover.

When there were only two shadow creatures left to defeat, Valentina rode straight for them.

"Didn't anyone ever teach you not to play with fire?" she asked breezily, as Cinder blasted them with an impressive display of magic fireballs.

The shadow creatures disappeared with a puff, fanning the enchanted flames. The flames flared, forming a ring of fire, trapping Valentina and her unicorn inside. Cinder let out a panicked neigh and rose up on his hind legs.

"Awww," called Crimsette, swooping above them. "It looks like someone's still learning how to use their new tricks!"

Valentina held on to Cinder's neck. For the first time, she didn't know what to do.

"This way!"

A bridge of rainbow light stretched itself over the fiery circle. Sophia and Wildstar were waiting on the other side. Light flowed from the unicorn's golden hooves – Wildstar had used her magic to create an escape route.

"Apparently now *you* need some help," grinned Sophia, as Valentina and Cinder galloped across to safety.

"Thank you," said Valentina. "And Sophia ... cool hair!"

Sophia smiled for a second, then Valentina hastily pulled herself up and added, "Not that this means we're friends!"

Working together had made the Unicorn Riders even stronger. Ravenzella realised that she would need to be more devious if she was going to ruin their island forever. She clenched her hands into claws, then summoned her most powerful Grim Magic. Thick shadow tendrils that whipped like snakes were suddenly sent lunging towards Sophia and Wildstar.

Bang!

Wildstar crashed her hoof to the ground, to change her rainbow into a diamond-hard shield of light. One by one the shadows tendrils hit the light and fizzled down to nothing. Ravenzella screamed in fury.

"That little trick might protect *you*," she spat, "but what about your precious friends..."

"No!" wailed Sophia. "No, you can't!"

The queen channelled all of her nastiness on Ava and the other Sapphire dorm students, thrilled to have discovered Sophia's weakness. Grim Magic swirled around Leaf, Glacier, Storm, Cinder and River, binding them in its darkness. The riders quickly jumped to the ground, watching in dismay as the unicorns they loved so much began to slowly shimmer away.

"Leaf!" gasped Ava, throwing her arms around her friend. "Please!"

Ravenzella cackled, ready for Sophia to give up and beg for mercy. To her surprise, the girl sounded more determined than ever.

"You're going to regret hurting my friends," Sophia promised her, carefully hiding her worry. She tapped the saddle and Wildstar reared up to

145

her full height, then charged at Ravenzella.

The queen was shocked, but not defeated. Quick as flash, she blasted a cloud of smoke into Sophia and Wildstar's faces. While they coughed and spluttered in the smog, she raced on towards Starglow Lake.

As soon as the air had cleared enough to see, Sophia and Wildstar galloped after the evil queen. They caught up with her at Unicorn Rock, a cliff at the top of a frothing waterfall that plunged into the lake below. Ravenzella's magic seemed unstoppable, but Sophia and her unicorn battled it with everything they had.

"You're a fool to think light could overpower my darkness," spat the queen, hurling barbs of Grim Magic in all directions. "My shadows will spread across the whole island. Say goodbye to your precious unicorns!"

The power of Ravenzella's spell pushed Sophia

and Wildstar towards the cliff edge. Sophia gasped as Wildstar stumbled and nearly fell down into the waterfall. The unicorn pulled herself back just in time.

Ravenzella sensed victory. "Your father took everything from me. I only wish he was here to see this!"

Sophia was pushed back a little further. But as she raised her chin to look Ravenzella in the eye, the clouds parted above them, revealing a single sparkling, shining star.

"Dad *is* here to see this," she said, with a smile.

Sophia and Wildstar's trust had never been stronger than this moment. The unicorn glowered at their enemy and her magical star markings began to glow opal-bright. Ravenzella watched, horrified, as the majestic creature pointed her spiralled horn up towards the sky, drawing in the light from the star. A channel of illuminous beams coursed downwards to the unicorn, dazzling in its brilliance.

"Now!" urged Sophia.

Ravenzella shrivelled back in fear, but there was nowhere to hide. Wildstar aimed her fantastically bright light at the Queen of Grimoria. *Whoosh!* Ravenzella was turned into solid stone. Sophia slid off the unicorn's back and watched as the stone figure wobbled and then toppled over the cliff edge. It hit the water in a blinding burst of light and sank to the very bottom of the lake.

"Wildstar!" sobbed Sophia, throwing her arms around her unicorn's neck. "We did it!"

Ravenzella was gone. All across the island, her Grim Magic was fading. Ash and Crimsette fled as the first beams of rainbow light shimmered through the academy, driving the shadows away. The unicorns, and their magic, were back.

SOPHIA'S INVITATION

The Unicorn Academy rang out with the sound of clapping and cheering. Teachers and students rushed through the gardens, eager to welcome back the triumphant Unicorn Riders. At the very same moment Ravenzella had been turned to stone, the unicorns had all been freed from her wicked spell. Now the friends huddled round Sophia and Wildstar, hugging and swapping tales of their adventures. Sophia touched her pendant and her heart swelled – this is what true friendship felt like.

"I'm so pleased you're OK," gushed Ava. "You beat the Queen of Grimoria!"

Valentina winked, before adding: "*With our help!*"

Sophia looked across at Wildstar, and then giggled. The friends strolled happily through the beautiful academy gardens, until Wildstar came to a sudden stop. The unicorn looked down

149

suspiciously at a pot of pink roses and snorted, her tail swishing left and right.

"Hmm..." said Rory, leaning over Storm's shoulder to get a better look. "I don't remember those flowers being there before."

Wildstar gently nudged the planter with her nose. The riders gasped as it somehow lifted itself up and scuttled backwards.

"Am I crazy or does that planter have legs?" exclaimed Ava.

The pot edged a little further back, stumbling into Leaf's hooves. The bump knocked the pot to the ground, revealing Fernakus hiding underneath.

Layla stared at him accusingly. "Where do you think you're going?"

"Petula, come!" shouted the Dwerpin.

The enchanted pig fluttered down and Fernakus hastily climbed onto her back.

"Let's get out of here!" he snapped.

Unfortunately for him, Petula wasn't in the mood to follow orders. She wriggled and shook Fernakus off, sending him rolling like a barrel towards Wildstar's hooves. Without the might of his nasty friends, he suddenly looked very small and very silly.

"What a delightfully dreamy day," said Sophia.

"Yes indeed!" spluttered Fernakus. "Well done, Unicorn Riders, I knew you could do—"

He didn't get to finish. Two Dwerpins hurried over, picked Fernakus up and carried him, kicking and arguing, away.

Layla crouched down to give Petula a lovely rub on her tummy.

"Good job!" she cooed.

Shortly after, Ms Primrose and Ms Furi came to greet the students.

"I must say, this class shows a great deal of potential," said Ms Primrose, looking at Sophia and her friends. "Well done."

Ms Furi nodded curtly. "Just remember we have rules here at Unicorn Academy, however. You broke several, and in the future, that will not be tolerated."

"Sometimes," said Ms Primrose, interrupting her, "rules are meant to be broken."

The headteacher looked at Sophia and winked, before guiding Ms Furi away. Sophia beamed.

The next day, as dawn began to break over Unicorn Island, Sophia went outside to get some air. She looked up at the pinky orange sunrise and took a deep breath. Wildstar clip-clopped steadily behind as she wandered through the academy courtyard. When Sophia found herself by her father's statue, which was glowing gently in the early morning sunlight, she sat down beside it.

"Well Dad, my first week here was pretty great," she said quietly. Wildstar lowered her head and nuzzled her gently. Sophia stroked the unicorn's neck and asked her, "Could I *actually* be a legendary Unicorn Rider like my dad one day?"

And as she gazed into Wildstar's eyes, searching, something truly magical happened.

"You will be, Sophia," said a low, gentle voice.

For a fleeting moment, a vision of her dad appeared. His face was there looking out at her, just as she remembered! Sophia blinked, and looked again, but the vision had gone.

"Is everything OK?"

Ava and Layla walked up, smiling.

"I think," whispered Sophia, "I just saw my dad."

And for the first time in a long time Sophia didn't feel sad. She had found her extraordinary ... and this was just the beginning.

✦ ✦ ✦

THE BOOKS THAT INSPIRED
THE NETFLIX SERIES!